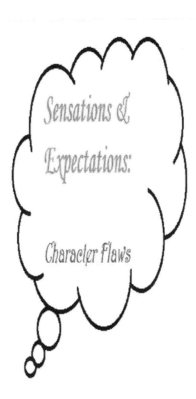

Sensations &
Expectations:

Character flaws

Sensations & Expectations
Character Flaws

-by Sandrana M. Wilson

My, my, my! Well, aren't we the quite inquisitive bunch of folks? As I can see you are quite indulgent as to what happened next with this colorful group of people, aren't you? Well, I'm going to go on and let you in on a few things about these individuals and give you a little insight on how their minds and bodies function.

We have our girl Shawna, who is the

main chick and the one who is going all out to come to terms with her sexuality and show that she is not only smart but sexy and damn sure won't back down to a challenge from anyone. Her ass is phat, tight, thick, however you like it and all the guys like to watch it but can't keep up so all they do is watch.

Allison was the guys' chick. The one every guy wanted to be with and desired because they didn't know if she wanted them or girls. She was mysterious in nature and super seductive when it came to dancing with her girls.

Patience and Elite were the girly

ones. Always dressy and flawless when they wore their makeup. They were the ones that guys would freak on and want to take for a spin afterwards, if you catch my drift.

Trina was the smaller, more flexible of the group. The girls would protect her from anyone trying to come up on her because they didn't want to have her fiancé Aaron fighting in the club or dealing with any mess.

Now all if the girls were very enticing and so damn fine, but something about them made them unforgettable. Each one had to a secret and only their group of friends knew what each one's secret was.

Having a great sense of humor only made them closer and sharing everything made their bond even stronger. Knowing everything and anything about who and what each one of them have done was why these women stayed friends and sisters in heart.

Shawna is the only one I will discuss in this story because for some reason she is the most open hearted and easy to read and please without pushing buttons. Plus, she wouldn't get mad if I tell her story and how she gets down, if you know what I mean.

I'm going to start off by saying that Shawna was the very athletic type in her teens and as she grew older she went from athletic to voluptuous over the years. Her body got thicker and men were beginning to notice and so was she.

She went from wearing shorts and t-shirts to tight fitted clothing that accentuated her curves and showed off her shape. Knowing how to entice and intimidate the opposite sex she became more in tune with herself and how to get what she wanted. The desire to want to be wanted by anyone she came across, grew strong in her and made her even more seductive in her ways.

After all, she didn't want her full-figure body to hinder her from being loved or make her feel like she wasn't beautiful. She knew she had a lot to offer and wanted to prove it no matter what.

When all of the girls would get together, Shawna would always have them meet in the same spot and they would go out and have a great time. This one particular weekend, she wanted them to catch a show and a bite to eat before they all joined the crew at the club.

Allison had to work four doubles back to back and was unable to join them but the show still went on. The girls and Aaron went out to the comedy show and had a bite to eat then departed before the night was over and headed to their usual spot.

The club was thick. People from out of town flocked to the dance floor and there was a crowd of people that flooded the area that the girls are usually cohabitating. They grabbed their drinks and headed over by the dance floor and spotted in the corner, grinding on some unknown, was the guy that Shawna shared one night with.

Trina warned Shawna about the ordeal and Shawna shrugged her shoulders and played it off as if she didn't care. The night went on and Shawna, Trina, Elite and Patience took over the dance floor and all eyes were on them.

Just like any other time, the girls' sexy style captivated this crowd too and the chick Shawna's lover was dancing with was now kicked to the curb. For some reason, his attention had steered toward the girls and Shawna didn't pay him any attention.

Elite and Patience had the attention of two young guys that had them damn near on the floor, like they were having sex and wanted them to submit to their every wish. Trina and Shawna were dancing like two sexy sirens and their dancing was so sultry that the men watching were hypnotized and in a trance.

Shawna glanced over and saw that she had indeed been watch by her friend and wanted to give him something to want over and over again. It wasn't hard for her to do, seeing that she wore knee high boots and a short dress that barely covered her ass. Plus she was dancing triple x rated.

"Did you see that shit?" Trina said to Shawna. "He just came over and tried to dance on you and you just moved. That shit was too funny."

"Oh, really?" Shawna replied. "That it too comical. I'm done with your boy."

The night went on and on and the girls had a great time doing them like they do all the time. Shawna said goodnight to Aaron and Trina. Patience and Elite were wasted and just wanted Shawna to take them home and Shawna was horny as ever from all of her sexy dancing and thinking about how she could do her lover in again.

Seeing that Shawna had an admirer the last time she had left the club, she didn't want to disappoint her newfound friend by not showing him that she was the type of chick to talk shit and not do anything about it. As she walked to her car, her admirer, the bouncer, ran up to her and grabbed her, lifter her up and landed a kiss dead smack on her lips.

She was in total shock and couldn't do anything but stand there. Her girls and everyone around her stared and cheered him on. The crowd gathered and all you heard was admiration of the boldness that he had shown. Everyone was amazed. Everyone, except for Shawna's former love interest. He looked a little pissed, if you ask me.

"Now that's a man. Go in for what he

wants and gets it," Elite and Patience said. "Yeah, I know what I want and your girl is it," he replied. Shawna was delighted. Blushing and feeling giddy, she almost stumbled walking through the parking lot.

"Girl! My heart is pounding so fast," she said to her friends. "He is a trip. Guess he showed him."

Well, I would say that Shawna wasn't going to fall for the games that these two were playing, but for some reason she was a little intrigued by the adventure. The fact that the one she slept with wasn't showing interest after their encounter and now that she had an admirer, he wants to get mad, really made her feel some type of way.

When Shawna got to her car there was a card and a note that read:

"I really want to get to know you and I hope I'm not being to straightforward but you really rock my world. Can we take this further and be more than friends? I want to be your man and do all the things that a real man is supposed to do for his woman...

Sincerely,

Christian"

So delighted that she saw the note, Christian walked up behind her and grabbed her and covered her eyes. Shawna was a tad bit nervous. Not knowing who it was she reached for their hands and slowly removed them and turned around. Not saying a word, she glanced into his eyes and smiled.

"So, are you going to give me an answer or are you going to look like a deer in headlights?" he said to her.

"Well," Shawna started, "I don't like to be surprised and you surely have shocked and amazed me tonight. I would love to be the woman on your arm."

Elated that she said yes, Christian picked her up in the air again and kissed her long and so passionate that he didn't want to let her go. He had her turn around and put a necklace around her neck that had their initials hanging from it.

Elite and Patience were so happy for Shawna. They wanted her to enjoy the rest of the night with him and offered to get rides home with some male friends that were standing around.

Seeing that Christian and Shawna had just made it official, he wanted to take her out to eat and treat his lady like the queen that she was. He took her to one of the best restaurants open that night. They invited their friends to join them to celebrate.

With everyone in attendance it made the night a more than joyous one for Christian and Shawna. "Now this is what I call a night to remember," Trina said. "You can say that again," Aaron said. "Nothing could ruin a lovely ending like this, not even a thunderstorm," Patience stated.

"I love all of y'all. No matter what goes down we always keep it real and I love that about us. I'm glad you came straight out and told me how you feel, Christian," Shawna said.

The night was get coming to an end and everyone was starting to leave the restaurant. Everyone said goodnight to Christian and Shawna and parted their ways. Well I would say that Shawna and Christian said goodnight to each other also but they had other intensions. They wanted to spend more time with each other and decided to take a ride in his car and go park on the east side of town to enjoy the sunrise.

Christian packed some blankets, bottled waters and a nice fruit basket for them to enjoy while they cuddled on the grass, watching the sun come up. Sitting there all alone in the park, he wrapped his arms around her and gave her a nice warm hug and whispered in her ear how much he really was pleased that she accepted his offer to be his queen.

There was nothing more romantic to her than this moment right here. Shawna couldn't even come up the words to speak, she was in so much of a shock. He was definitely her prince charming and her dream was coming true. She had become the fairytale princess that she had only read about and dreamed of being.

There wasn't anything or anyone that could ruin this moment and God knows she needed him in her life. Christian wasn't trying to force himself on her. He wasn't trying to have sex with her. He wanted to just be with her and make her feel wanted for who she was, his queen for him to protect and love.

Sensations &
Expectations:

Lovers' Triangle

21

Sensations & Expectations

Lovers' Triangle

-by Sandrana M. Wilson

Now that Shawna and Christian had made it official and have confirmed with each other that they were for one another, they were determined to get to really know each other.

Christian always adored the cute way that Shawna would dress and her demeanor was one like no other. She was unique and he loved every bit of her.

A week flew by and it felt like an

eternity. They kept in touch via chat, email, text, and phone calls. These two lovebirds can't seem to live without hearing that the other was doing fine.

Well Shawna wanted to get everyone together for a night on the town and Christian had to work.

It was Aaron's birthday weekend and everyone had agreed to bring a dish to enjoy for the party. As a surprise for his party, Elite asked a few of her friends to dress up in their sexy outfits and perform a strip show.

Everything was going according to plan and the only things missing were the presence of Allison and

Patience.

Where had these two been? For the
past two weeks Allison had a lot of
things going on with her boyfriend
and his mom. She found out that his
mom was diagnosed with cancer and
with her having an aunt that died
from lung and breast cancer, this
really hit home.

Patience did not seem to want to be
bothered with anyone. She was
secretive, but Shawna knew
everything that was going on with
her.

Patience was caught up in a lover's
triangle. Two guys that she had a
threesome with were starting to

come on strong and wanted to become more than friends with benefits with her. They wanted to be her man and neither one of them knew of the intentions of the other.

Now this was the first time that Patience had encountered this problem. Well damn, that was the first time she had a threesome.

For her to take on more than one man at one time, this was legendary. Seeing that she had the option of making both of them her playmates, she was a bit turned on.

With the desire to play the field and do whatever and whomever she wanted, Patience took it upon herself to play the damsel in distress.

She called up the first guy, Daniel, and told him that she really needed him to come by her house and help her with some plumbing.

Now Daniel couldn't catch on that she was trying to get him in her house to see him naked. He actually thought that she was in need of some real plumbing.

When he reached Patience's house, he noticed that there was a car in her driveway. Daniel could not help but wonder what exactly was Patience up to, so he peeped into her bedroom window and saw Nathan, the other guy that they had a threesome with, in her bed with only his boxers on.

Without asking her what was going on, he jumped back in his car and began to text Patience that he won't be able to come through and that she should call a plumber.

Patience was in shock. She thought that surely she had this one in the bag.

She called Daniel back and asked him why he had the sudden change of heart. Daniel was so sure that Patience was trying to play him. He knew what he saw and Nathan was in her bedroom and to make matters worse, he was in his boxers.

Quite obvious to the onlookers, I'd say. I would think that Patience would have been a little bit more discreet in her actions, seeing that she knew both of them wanted more than one night of passion out of her.

Well not all women get the rush that she was experiencing. So let's see how this plays out for the three of them.

Will Patience end up wrapped in the firm arms of Nathan, again or will Daniel proclaim his love for her and give her the love that she has been thriving for?

Well... Let's find out.

While Daniel tried to come up with excuses as to why he left, he couldn't help but think over and over about Nathan being in Patience's bedroom.

His anger overcame him and at that very moment he raised his voice and let out everything that he was thinking.

(Daniel furious)

"What the fuck is your problem?" You called me sounding like you really had a problem with your pipes and as a fuckin courtesy to you, I actually come over.What the fuck I look like doing something for you when you can't even be honest? Is that who the fuck you're fuckin with now?"

(Patience startled)

"Please!!! Just hear me out!"

(Daniel)

"What the hell is there to listen to? I think what I saw speaks more to me than any words. I should have left it as it was...a piece of ass that wanted two dicks to get her pussy wet."

Daniel couldn't bring himself to even look at her. To him, she meant more to him than just a threesome. He wanted so much more. This is the one woman that he felt he could make his own.

Patience fucked up every chance that she had at getting her panties wet by the same two men who fulfilled her threesome fantasy. The little games that she tried to play had come full circle and fucked her over.

ABOUT THE AUTHOR:

SANDRANA WILSON

****

Sandrana Wilson is an ambitious
mother, lover, friend, and above all

writer who is very passionate about her work. She has written several pieces of work that range from songs, poems, cartoon strips and stories, just to name a few. If you want a passionate writer who expresses love and desire in such a way that you get engulfed into the characters or the words of some of her work, you have found her.

She finds herself making her friends and family laugh or smile even when they are down. She loves the idea of love and peace so much that her words just overflow with desire. Some may even call her the Aphrodite of this day and age. Her words captivate men and women alike and can make people fall in love with the desire and inspirations of their hearts.

Keep your eyes wide open and see that what Sandrana has to offer is more than a story, but a seductive roll that all of us would like to play.

****

Made in the USA
Middletown, DE
18 April 2023

28832456R00021